Transportation & Communication Series

Fire Engines

Arlene Bourgeois Molzahn

Enslow Publishers, Inc.

40 Industrial Road   PO Box 38
Box 398   Aldershot
Berkeley Heights, NJ 07922   Hants GU12 6BP
USA   UK

http://www.enslow.com

To my grandchildren Nicole and Kyle and their Uncle Mike who is a firefighter.

Library of Congress Cataloging-in-Publication Data

Molzahn, Arlene Bourgeois.
    Fire engines / Arlene Bourgeois Molzahn.
        p. cm. — (Transportation & communication series)
    Includes bibliographical references and index.
    ISBN 0-7660-1643-9
    1. Fire engines—Juvenile literature. 2. Fire extinction—Juvenile
literature. [1. Fire engines. 2. Fire extinction. 3. Fire fighters.]
I. Title. II. Series.
    TH9372 .M65   2001
    628.9'25—dc21   00-011260

Printed in the United States of America

10 9 8 7 6 5 4 3 2 1

To Our Readers:
All Internet Addresses in this book were active and appropriate when we went to press. Any comments or suggestions can be sent by e-mail to Comments@enslow.com or to the address on the back cover.

Every effort has been made to locate all copyright holders of materials used in this book. If any errors or omissions have occurred, corrections will be made in future editions of this book.

Photo Credits: Sean F. Cassidy, pp. 12, 13, 14, 15, 26 (bottom), 34, 35, 40; Corel Corporation, pp. 10, 16, 17, 18, 22, 23, 24, 27 (bottom), 28, 29 (top), 30, 31, 32 (bottom), 33, 36, 37, 38 (bottom) , 41 (top), 42, 43; Dover Publications, p. 20; Hemera Technologies, Inc. 1997-2000, pp. 1, 2, 5, 6, 11, 19, 21, 25, 29 (bottom), 32, 39, 41 (bottom); Library of Congress, pp. 4, 7, 8, 26 (top), 27 (top), 32 (top).

Cover Illustration: Sean F. Cassidy

Contents

Chapter 1

Fire Everywhere

Fires start in many ways. Most fires are caused because people are not careful. Some fires, such as those that start from earthquakes or lightning, are caused by nature.

By 1906, San Francisco was a big city in California. People liked its mild winter weather. Some liked the beautiful mountains nearby. Others liked being near the Pacific Ocean. These are all good things about the city.

But, San Francisco is a city that sometimes has earthquakes. Many of the buildings in the

Horses pulled steam engines in the 1900s. But no amount of fire-fighting power would help San Francisco in 1906.

5

city were made of wood. Wooden buildings can move a little without falling down. They can stand earthquakes better than those made of brick. Brick buildings fall quickly when the earth moves. But wooden buildings burn much easier and faster.

Early in the morning of April 18, 1906, the people of San Francisco heard a strange low rumbling noise. Then the earth began to shake. Soon the noise of glass breaking and houses crashing down filled the air. A giant earthquake had hit the city. Gas lines were broken when the earth moved. Power wires were also broken. This caused sparks that set the gas on fire. The fires began as soon as the ground stopped moving. Fires started everywhere.

The earthquake broke water pipes in the city. It also broke the pipes that carried water to the city. Soon the firemen could not get water to put out the fires. All they could do was build a firebreak. A firebreak is made by

A giant earthquake hit San Francisco, California on April 18, 1906. It caused many fires (right).

moving away all of the things that can burn. When a fire has nothing left to burn it goes out. So the firemen began to blow up buildings ahead of the fire. Then they burned the buildings to make a firebreak. This helped keep the fire from spreading. But it did not put out all the fires.

The fires lasted for two days and nights. Over 600 people died because of the fires. Over 3,000 people were hurt. The fires burned 28,000 buildings that cost about $350 million. Houses on over 500 city blocks were burned down before the fire ended. Thousands of people were left without homes.

Soon people started to build new buildings in the burned part of the city. Most of them did not use wood. In a few years, the city of San Francisco was built up again. But the 1906 earthquake and fires in San Francisco will always be remembered.

Over 28,000 buildings, and houses on more than 500 city blocks, were burned down before the fires ended.

Chapter 2

Kinds of Fire-Fighting Engines

There are three kinds of fire engines. Most big fire stations have fire engine trucks, ladder trucks, and rescue trucks.

Fire engine trucks are sometimes called pumper trucks. This is because they have large water pumps on them. These pumps push water through the hoses onto the fire.

Some fire engines are made for putting out small grass fires. These trucks carry a large tank of water with them. They also carry shovels and rakes.

Ladder trucks are another kind of fire engine. There are two kinds of ladder trucks.

Some fire engines have a panel (left) like this one.

One ladder truck is called an aerial ladder truck. It has a long ladder. When the ladder is stretched out it can reach up to ten stories high. With these ladders, firefighters can get near a fire burning in a very tall building. They can also use these ladders to save people and pets that are trapped in a tall building.

The other kind of ladder truck is called an elevating platform truck, or snorkel. It also has a very long ladder. The ladder is built in two or three parts.

This pumper truck is ready to go.

Ladder trucks carry different size ladders, saws, and other tools to help firefighters get into a burning building.

These parts can be folded or unfolded to reach a fire. A cage, or bucket, is at the top of the ladder. Firefighters can stand in the bucket and spray water on places that are hard to reach.

Rescue trucks are another kind of fire truck. They carry special tools that might be needed at a fire. Sometimes firefighters need to get into a house. Rescue trucks carry tools to break down doors or to break windows. They also have tools for cutting through metal. In

All of the special gear that firefighters need is neatly stored on a fire engine. The hoses fold up on the side of the truck.

A heavy rescue truck at a fire. Rescue trucks carry special cameras, water rescue gear, and air tanks.

the rescue trucks are small tools like jacks for lifting or moving things. They also have saws, ropes, and axes, which are sometimes needed at fires. Some fires cannot be put out with water, such as grease fires. Fire engines carry special foams and powders to put out those kinds of fires.

A Crash Rescue Vehicle, or CRV, is another kind of rescue fire truck. It can travel over all types of land. When an airplane crashes far away from roads, a CRV can reach it quickly.

Fireboats are boats that can fight fires from the water. These boats have large pumps. They put out fires on ships. They can also spray water on a building that is burning close to the shore. Two other kinds of fire-fighting vehicles

Fireboats fight fires from the water. They help to put out fires in buildings close to the water and on boats.

Tanker fire engines are used where there are no fire hydrants. Tankers supply pumper trucks with water.

Fire-fighting planes (right) drop special chemicals to put out fires.

Fire-fighting helicopters scoop up water and drop it on a fire. The bucket can be seen to the left of the helicopter on the ground.

are the fire-fighting helicopter and the fire-fighting airplane.

The fire-fighting helicopter carries a huge bucket of water. It drops the water on the fire. Then it goes back for more water.

A fire-fighting airplane has a tank under the body of the plane. The plane flies down to just the top of a lake, or other large body of water. It fills the tank by scooping up the water as it flies along. Then the airplane flies to the fire and drops the water. Fire-fighting airplanes and helicopters can be used in fighting forest fires.

Chapter 3

Early Fire Fighting

Long ago there were no fire engines or firefighters. When people saw a fire, they quickly grabbed buckets and ran to the fire. They made two teams and each team formed a long line from the fire to the nearest well or river. People filled the buckets with water. Then one line passed the buckets of water from person to person until the buckets reached the fire. The water was poured on the fire. Then the other line of people sent the buckets back to be filled again. This was called the bucket brigade. The bucket brigade did not

These firefighters work to put this fire out using old fire engines.

put out many fires, but it did keep the fire from reaching other buildings.

The first fire engine in America did not have an engine. It looked like a wooden box on wheels. Men had to pull it to a fire. A pump on the wooden box pushed the water through a short hose. It took twenty-eight men to

This poster is from the 1890s. It shows the Remington Hose Cart. The horses seem to be running around the cart to make the water pump through the hoses.

make the pump work. A bucket brigade was needed to keep the wooden box filled with water. This fire engine did not work very well.

In 1829, the first steam fire engine was built. Years later after it was made better, the steam fire engine became popular. City people liked this fire engine. It could spray water to the top of buildings. It needed only three men to make the pump work. The job of one fireman was to yell at people to get out of the way. Horses were needed to pull this fire engine. The horses were kept at the fire station. They needed to be ready to pull the fire engine day or night.

By 1910, some cities had fire engines that had gasoline engines. They carried tools for fighting fires such as ladders, long hoses, shovels, and axes. The fire engines were always painted red. They had open cabs. The firefighters would hang on to the sides of the truck as they went to a fire. One fireman rang

Horses were needed at a moments notice to pull the early fire engines.

a bell to tell the people to get out of the way. Another fireman cranked the fire siren by hand so people could hear the truck coming. The new trucks were slow and often broke down. But they were faster than horses.

Firefighters were very proud of these fire engines. They worked hard to keep them shining and running well. City people were also very proud of their fire engines. In the early days, fire engines were almost always the best part of a city parade.

Soon better fire engines were built. The cabs were covered. The firefighters sat inside the trucks. Loud electric sirens were put on all fire engines. People could hear them coming from far away. The new trucks were much bigger. They could carry more and better tools to fight fires. They were much faster. They could reach a fire in time to save a building from burning down.

As fire engines became better, firefighters were able to get to a fire faster (left).

Before bells and sirens like these were put on fire engines, firefighters had to yell to people to get out of the way.

Chapter 4

Early Fire Engines

The first wooden pumper fire engines were made in England. They were brought across the ocean to cities in the United States.

John F. Rogers lived in the United States. In 1832, he built a pumper fire engine. He started a company called Rogers Patent Balance Fire Engine. Later, other companies were started. Then all the companies got together and made

Horses were used to pull steam fire engines in the 1800s.

Some early fire engines used steam to make them move, but most were pulled by horses.

Atlantic Highlands, New Jersey's Engine 86-77 is an old Mack pumper truck.

one big company. This big company was called the American Fire Engine Company. It made most of the pumper fire engines for the United States at that time.

Other small companies started making the ladders and long hoses for firefighters to use. But fire engines and fire wagons were still pulled by horses.

In 1904, the Merryweather Company in England built the first fire engine with a gasoline motor. It carried a large tank for water. It also carried hoses, ladders, and fire extinguishers. Today this fire engine is in the London Science Museum.

In 1906, the Waterous Engine Works built the first American-made fire engine with a gasoline motor. The bright red fire engine was bought by the city of Wayne, Pennsylvania. The Seagrave Company, Ahrens-Fox, and American La France were builders of early fire engines with gas engines.

In the early 1920s, most cities began to buy fire engines with motors in them. These fire engines were faster than horses. But the fire engines often broke down. Cities sold their horses and got new fire engines anyway. Very few people in 1920 knew how to drive a car or truck. So all the new fire engines came with a book. The book was to help the firefighters learn to drive the fire engine. At first the firemen were not very good drivers. But

Before steam or gasoline engines were popular, fire trucks were pulled by horses.

The Seagrave Company built many early fire engines, like this 1914 pumper truck.

they quickly learned how to drive. Many small companies began making fire engines. They learned how to make them work better. By 1930, nearly every city had fire engines with motors in them.

In the 1930s fire engines did not break down as often. Some firefighters had learned how motors worked. They could fix the trucks when they broke down. Firefighters had also become very good drivers. By that time, some companies were putting closed cabs on the

Just like the new cars at the time, in 1919, the fire engines did not have tops or windows.

fire engines. This kept the driver warm in winter and dry when it rained. But the other firefighters still had to ride in the open air on the sides and back of the truck. They were often cold and wet.

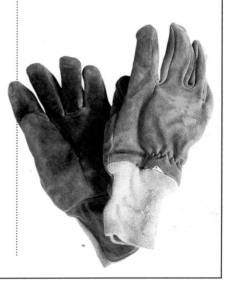

Very few fire engines were made in the 1940s because of World War II. All the companies were building vehicles for the United States Army. After the war ended, fire engines were made stronger. They were made to go faster. They had cabs for the drivers. They also had places inside the trucks for the rest of the firefighters.

All fire engines were once painted red. Today some are still red but many are painted a lime green or a yellow color. Firefighters want everyone to see them coming. They are trying to find the color that is easiest for people to see.

Fire engines have to be a bright color so they are easy to see. Fire engines are usually painted red, lime green, or yellow.

Chapter 5

All Kinds of Jobs

The job of fighting fires has become a full-time job in the United States. Even people living in small cities and in the country have firefighters working to keep them safe.

Some firefighters live at the fire station. They eat and sleep there. If there is a fire, they work hard to put it out. On days when there are no fires to put out, they work on the fire engines. They keep them shining clean. They make sure the engines are running well.

Many people work to make things that are used by firefighters. Fire engine companies make all kinds of trucks needed for different

Many people work together to make sure firefighters wear the right gear. These firefighters (left) are wearing their special helmets and coats.

Even in early 1900s, fire-fighters kept their fire engines shining clean.

These firefighters sit around a table eating at their fire station. If they are called to a fire, they have to get ready quickly.

kinds of fires. There are trucks made to fight fires when an airplane crashes. Some trucks are made to take people who are hurt or sick to a hospital. Special cars are made for the fire chief so that he can race to a fire.

Firefighters need boots, helmets, coats, and pants. Face masks and air tanks are also needed. They use new cameras that can see through smoke and ladders that are lighter and stronger. Firefighters need large fans to pull the smoke out of buildings after a small fire has been put out. Many people have jobs making the things needed by firefighters in the United States and around the world.

Some people have jobs making things that help to keep our homes safe from fire. Smoke

Dispatchers are very important. They tell the firefighters where to go to fight a fire.

Fire chiefs need to get to a fire fast. They are in charge of the firefighters that are putting out a fire.

alarms are made to alert us when there is smoke in our house. Ladders are made that are easy to carry. They can be hooked on to an outside window. If there is a fire, people can climb down from a second floor without being hurt. Fire extinguishers are made to put out very small fires. Some people work making clothes that do not burn quickly.

Workers make foam to use when water cannot be used to put out a fire.

Some people work in machine shops that make fire hydrants. These must be easy for firefighters to open. Most big cities have workers who keep the fire hydrants painted so that they are easy to see. These workers also

Firefighters use many different types of trucks. This ambulance is ready to take people to the hospital.

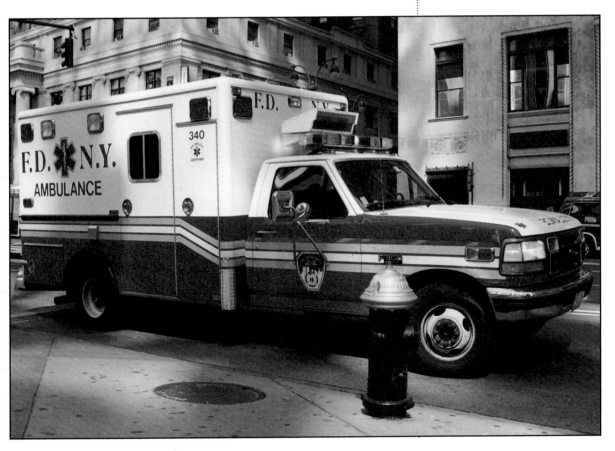

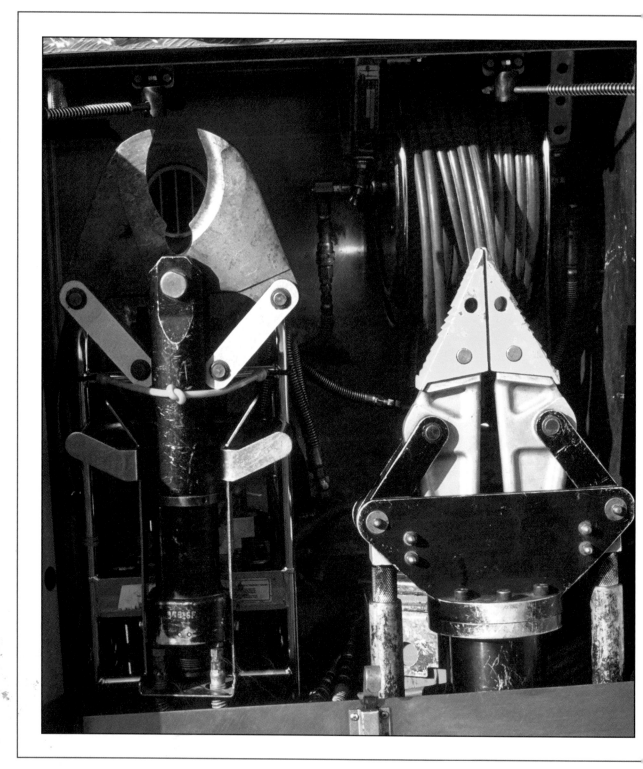

make sure that the hydrants are ready for firefighters to use.

Some workers make lifesaving machines. Some machines help people when they are having a heart attack. Other machines help people to breathe. These machines help firefighters save people who are sick or hurt.

Many people work to help firefighters keep us safe.

Firefighters might use the "Jaws of Life" (left) to cut through metal to rescue people who are trapped.

Firefighters may need oxygen tanks to help them breathe when they are fighting smoky fires.

Chapter 6

Newer and Better

Today Pierce Manufacturing of Wisconsin is the biggest company that makes fire engines in the United States. Cities from all over the world buy their fire engines from Pierce Manufacturing. This company does not build every fire engine the same way. It finds out just what a city wants the fire engine to do. Then it builds it to do all those things.

Many things are being changed on fire engines. All new fire engines will be made to carry foam for putting out fires. Then all fire engines will be able to spray foam on special kinds of fires.

Hoses (left) have to connect to the fire engine. Usually many hoses are used at once. People have to make sure the hoses work well.

Buckets, like this one, help firefighters get close to a fire so they can put the fire out.

The cages, or buckets, on the platform ladder trucks are going to be made bigger and stronger. Then more firefighters will be able to use the bucket at the same time.

Pierce Manufacturing is making trucks that do not rust. This will make fire engines last much longer.

No one knows what fire engines will look like in the future. But we do know that companies that make fire engines are always trying to make them better. They are trying to

find faster ways to put out fires. They are trying to make fire fighting safer for the firefighters.

After a fire stops burning, firefighters try to find out why the fire started. Fire engines carry many special tools that are used to look over burned buildings. They want to make sure that a fire will not start that way again. Each year new and better ways are found to keep fires from starting.

Today, some firefighters go to schools to talk to children about fire safety. Some look over large buildings and factories to make sure they are safe from fires.

Firefighters teach campers how to make safe campfires because forest fires are very hard to put out. Others fly in small airplanes over the forests. They look for signs of fire. They want to put out any fire as soon as it starts. Small fires are easier to

Firefighters work hard to put out forest fires.

Some firefighters go to schools to talk about fire safety. Others make sure fire extinguishers work well.

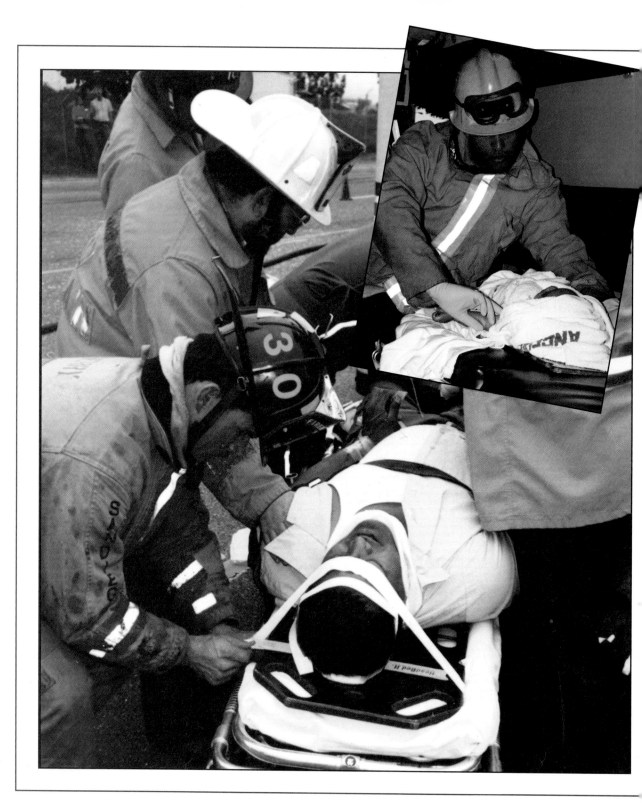

put out. Firefighters hope that someday new and better ways will be found to fight forest fires.

Most firefighters go to training school every year. They learn new and better ways of being safe while fighting a fire. They learn how to use new fire engines and how to use the new tools that fire engines carry. They learn new ways to fight fires.

Many years ago, most people felt that only men could be firefighters. Firefighters were called firemen because there were no women firefighters. Today many women are firefighters. They fight fires side by side with men. Perhaps more women will become firefighters in the future. Everyone should be thankful for the great job that men and women firefighters do to help us.

Firefighters not only put out fires, they also know how to save lives (left).

Firefighters have to work as a team to put a fire out.

Timeline

1600s–1700s—People use bucket brigades to fight fires. The first fire engine is like a wooden box on wheels.

1829—The first steam engine is built.

1832—John F. Rogers builds a fire truck pumper.

1904—Merryweather Company, England, builds the first fire engine with a gasoline motor.

1906—Waterous Engine Works builds the first American-made fire engine with a gasoline motor.

1930s—Nearly every city has fire engines with gasoline motors.

1940s—Few fire engines are made because the United States enters World War II in 1941.

1970s—Fire departments begin to hire women as firefighters.

2000—Companies are making bigger and better changes to fire engines.

Words to Know

cab—The place where the driver sits in a truck.

extinguisher—A tool used to put out fires.

fire hydrant—A pipe or water line from which firefighters pump up water.

firebreak—An area that is cleared of anything that can burn.

helmet—A kind of hard hat used by firefighters and other people who work in dangerous areas.

oxygen—A gas found in the air that is needed for fire to burn.

pump—Something that forces water or air in or out of things.

rescue—To save someone or something.

siren—A kind of whistle that makes a very loud noise.

Learn More About
Fire Engines

Books

Bingham, Caroline. *Fire Truck*. New York: DK
Publishing, 1995.

Budd, E.S. *Fire Engines*. Chanhassen, Minn.: The
Child's World, Inc., 1999.

Flanagan, Alice K. *Ms. Murphy Fights Fires*.
Danbury, Conn.: Children's Press, 1997.

Goldberg, Jan. *Fire Fighter*. Danbury, Conn.:
Children's Press, 1998.

Kallen, Stuart A. *The Fire Station*. Edina, Minn.:
ABDO Publishing Co., 1997.

Kuklin, Susan. *Fighting Fires*. New York: Aladdin
Paperbacks, 1999.

Otfinoski, Steve. *To the Rescue*. Tarrytown, N. Y.:
Marshall Cavendish Corp., 1999.

Learn More About
Fire Engines

Where to Write

International Association of Fire Fighters
1750 New York Avenue NW
Washington, D.C. 20006

National Fire Protection Association
1 Batterymarch Park
Quincy, MA 02269

Internet Addresses

Illinois Firesafe Kids

<http://www.state.il.us/kids/fire/fireman.htm>
Check out the House of Hazards to learn about fire safety in your home.

Sparky's Home Page

<http://www.sparky.org>
Sparky the Fire Dog® teaches fire safety. This is a fun site!

U.S. Fire Administration (USFA) Kids Place

<http://www.usfa.fema.gov/kids/>
This is "where the fun starts." Learn about fire safety. Become a Junior Fire Marshal.

Index